Discover other titles by John McDonnell at Amazon.com or Smashwords.com.

John McDonnell's Facebook: https://www.facebook.com/john.mcdonnell2

DEDICATION

Dedicated to my wife Anita for her eternal support, and to my amazing children.

TABLE OF CONTENTS

THE BEAUTY PART

"Don't accept rejection," that's always been my motto. It's a good motto for a beauty contestant, don't you think?

You can overcome anything if you don't believe in rejection.

I've been getting judged since I was eight years old and I entered my first pageant. I learned how to smile, to walk, and to answer all the questions right. I won just about every pageant I entered.

And the ones I didn't win? If you think about it long enough, you can figure out a reason for every one of Life's so-called rejections, and then it makes you feel better, and you can go on to yet another victory.

As an example, take my marriage.

I married Todd when I was 21 and still in college (paid for with my pageant scholarships!). He worshipped me, and he told me I looked like a goddess in my wedding gown. He just adored me, and we were very happy for a year or so.

Then, things changed.

Todd didn't seem as affectionate, and he found fault with me sometimes. Just little things, like that I never did any work around the house, and that I was too preoccupied with my appearance (it takes work to look like this, I always told him).

Well, I thought he'd come around eventually -- men have always loved me, so why wouldn't he?

There was another part, though. He was seeing someone. I found love letters from her, little gifts she'd given him, the scent of her perfume on his clothing.

I didn't handle it well, I admit. I got very angry at Todd. He denied it, but I could see in his eyes that he was lying.

Looking back, I acted foolishly. I took an overdose of sleeping pills. I know, it was a silly thing to do. I just wasn't thinking right, though.

Long story short, I slept for a long time.

And then I woke up.

And I had the answer.

Todd wasn't rejecting me, Sally Withersfield; he was rejecting Sally Withersfield, beauty queen. He was intimidated by my beauty, charm, and poise. The poor boy, he simply didn't see the real me. He didn't know the girl underneath the beauty queen; the girl beneath the skin.

Well, I'm not one to lie around when I've figured something out. First thing I wanted to do was go see Todd and tell him, make him see that I was not this intimidating beauty queen, I was just a normal flesh-and-blood girl.

It was nighttime, and nothing looked familiar, because I was still in a fog from all the sleeping pills, but I started off to find Todd.

I was moving slowly, and I walked and walked for what seemed like hours, but finally I found myself on our street, and I made my way to our house, at the end of a cobblestone drive next to the old church and the cemetery.

I decided to surprise Todd, so I let myself in quietly, and climbed the stairs. Wouldn't he be surprised when he saw me? I couldn't wait to see the look on his face.

I got to the bedroom and decided not to knock, to make the surprise better.

When I opened the door and turned on the light I had the shock of my life. There was my Todd in bed with another woman.

And not an attractive one, either -- she was nothing compared to me. Short, dumpy, and with wide set eyes and a mouth that was opened in a scream.

Well, of course the two of them were screaming -- who wouldn't be when they're caught in that position?

Something in Todd's eyes looked odd, though. He was looking at me with horror.

I wanted to reassure him that I had it all figured out. I wanted to explain everything, because I knew that as soon as I forgave him he'd understand and want me back. I wanted to tell him that everything was going to be all right.

I walked over to the bed, and they both scrambled to get away from me. I reached out to Todd, but he swatted my hand away.

And that's when the strangest thing happened.

My hand, with my whole arm attached, fell on the floor.

I stood there looking at it for a long time. It was brownish gray, with little white worms in it. Pretty as could be!

Then I picked it up with my other hand and reattached it.

You have to make the best of things, I always say. Be positive. Don't accept rejection.

Todd will see that in time. He's still talking to himself in the corner, but he'll come around eventually. The girl, well, she passed away, I'm afraid. I guess some people have weaker hearts than others.

The main thing is, now Todd has seen the real me.

And the beauty part is, it's been a real eye-opener for him.

THE END

STUCK

You know how you get a thought that you can't get out of your head? Your mind is stuck on it, like a song that plays over and over.

That's what was happening to him.

He couldn't stop thinking this one thought.

It wasn't supposed to be this way. He was engaged to be married, hadn't looked at another woman in so long. His fiancée was out of town -- what was her name again? No matter, it was Maya he wanted to think about.

He'd gone to the party with some friends. From the moment he walked in the door and saw Maya, the auburn hair, the green eyes, the way she laughed at everything -- he felt something change.

She told him she liked guys who took chances. "You look like somebody who takes chances," she said.

He smiled at that because it was so wrong. He was not a risk taker. He was an actuary, and he spent his days calculating risks for an insurance company. In his personal life he liked sure things. He had his life all planned out, even to how many children he'd have and where he'd spend his retirement thirty years from now. It was satisfying to plan that way.

"I never plan," she said. "Too boring. I want every moment to be different."

They talked for hours, and everything around them fell away. He was not aware of anyone else, of other conversations, of the time passing. Before long they were walking outside, where he kissed her under a willow tree in the moonlight. He knew he'd had too much to drink, but he couldn't resist. Just this once, he thought. Just this once I'll be crazy, wild, throw caution to the wind. Her kisses were electric, unlike anything he'd ever experienced. He felt himself letting go.

"I have a great idea," she said. "Let's go swimming in the quarry."

"I don't like to swim. I can't float."

"Oh, come on, don't be a spoilsport. It's great fun."

Then they were driving along a deserted road in his sensible car with the windows down and her hair streaming in the wind, and she was urging him to go faster.

"Come on, she said. "Push it. Isn't it fun? We're all alone; let's have some fun. Go faster."

He'd had too much to drink. One minute he was laughing and singing with her at the top of his lungs, feeling full of life, and the next he saw the tree, the big oak tree at a fork in the road, and he knew he couldn't stop in time -- it was all a picture, the most vivid picture he'd ever seen, just so clear. The tree, the car, the moonlight. Clear and sharp.

He couldn't get it out of his head.

Maybe that's why he went back to it every night, back to the twisted wreckage, the motor racing even though the car was wrecked, her screaming, scrambling out of the car through the passenger window, blood and makeup and tears streaking her face.

And his broken, bloody, mangled body lying there. It was the Other now. Dead, gone, all the plans turned to ashes.

The picture was stuck in his head and it kept repeating, over and over.

Forever.

THE END

THE THING IN THE BASEMENT

"Watch out for the thing in the basement," Billy's Uncle Hank used to say. He thought it was funny, and he'd smile when he told Billy about it. "Been down there a long time, since before I bought this house," he'd say. "People told me about it, told me not to buy the house, but I didn't listen. I know it's there, though -- I can feel its presence. Like a cold, clammy feeling; it makes your skin crawl. You know something's watching you, just waiting to pounce."

Billy didn't like his uncle. He was strange, had too many rules, and every rule had a punishment. The worst punishment was the basement. If you ever did something really bad, Uncle said, you would have to go downstairs where the thing lived.

The basement was called a "Michigan basement". It was unfinished, with a bare earth floor and walls. There was a workbench, with tools scattered all around, and clutter everywhere. Old, broken furniture. Ancient toys. Old magazines moldering in stacks. A bare lightbulb in the ceiling. It smelled damp and musty, and there were strange noises that came from the shadows. His uncle came down here to do his woodworking, and he had an assortment of saws, lathes, and chisels. There was even a big industrial table saw that could cut thick planks of wood.

When Billy's mother told him she was going away on vacation with his father and that he'd have to stay with his uncle for a week, he pleaded not to go.

"Now, Billy," his mother said. "You're being unreasonable. We can't afford to hire a babysitter for you for the week, and we have no other close relatives living nearby. We're not really friendly with any of our neighbors (you know I don't believe in getting chummy with neighbors), so Uncle Hank is the only option we have. I don't know why you keep saying you don't like your Uncle Hank. Why, he's my brother -- we're so close, we could almost be twins."

The first day, Billy broke a rule. His uncle had a strict rule about not wasting anything, and Billy accidentally tipped a liter bottle of soda over on the kitchen table, and all the soda poured out.

His uncle got red in the face, smiled, and said, "Well, Billy, I think for that infraction you need to spend some time in the basement."

Billy begged him not to go, but his uncle didn't listen. He grabbed Billy by the collar and marched him down the old wooden steps, then marched back up himself, closed the big wooden door and bolted it shut.

And then he turned out the light.

It was a good thing the house was set back from the road, and there were no neighbors close by, or they would have heard Billy's screams. Billy's uncle seemed not to notice the screams, or the pounding on the door, or any of the other noises that came from the basement. The next morning he came down to breakfast whistling a cheery tune. When he was finished eating his cereal, he said, "Well, Billy, I think you've had enough punishment for one night. Let's see how you're doing."

When Billy's mother got back from her trip and came to pick him up, she rang the doorbell over and over, but nobody answered. She tried the front door handle and found that the door was unlocked. She made her way through the house calling, "Billy, Hank, where are you?" In the kitchen she saw a cereal box on the sideboard, and a bowl and spoon in the sink.

The door to the basement was open.

She went downstairs slowly, calling, "Billy, Hank? Are you there?"

It was dark in the basement, and it took several moments before her eyes adjusted.

There was something at the far end of the room, by the table saw.

The thing in the basement moved toward her.

"Mama," it said.

THE END

THE BOX

"I will give you one hundred dollars for it," the woman said, swatting lazily at a fly that came too close to her in the dark shop.

"Are you mad?" the man said. He was red-faced and sweating, mopping his brow with a handkerchief. "It's 18th dynasty, I'm sure. Look at that, it's polished ebony, black as the Devil's hide. It's worth a thousand times what you're offering."

"No, professor. You know as well as I that it was stolen many years ago. You could not sell this on the open market. Besides, I know of this box. I have heard stories. It brings bad luck."

"Nonsense, you don't believe that rot, Nekhbet. You're too jaded for that. I admit the man who sold it to me had a haunted look in his eyes, but it was probably from his dissolute life."

"Is that so? I notice you are perspiring, professor. Could it be you have been drinking too much again?"

"A drop now and then, Nekhbet, purely for medicinal purposes. As it happens, though, I have a powerful thirst at the moment. Now about this box -- I am anxious to settle this. How much will you give me for it?"

"I could offer less, but because you are my friend, I will give you a hundred dollars. Not a penny more."

"Outrageous!" the professor said. "I paid triple that. You're insulting me. I'm going to take it right now and find someone who knows the value of an artifact like this."

His hand trembled when he reached for the box.

Nekhbet smiled.

Finally, the professor said, "Oh, hang it, woman, if I didn't need a drink desperately this very minute, I'd be off like a flash. You have me at a disadvantage, however, so I'll take it."

Nekhbet reached below the counter, unlocked a safe, and brought out a wad of money. She counted out a hundred and handed it to the professor, who grabbed the money and hurried out the door without saying goodbye.

Nekhbet put white linen gloves on and carefully stowed the box away under the counter. She had no desire to open it now. She would keep it till the next person, following the trail of whispers on the black market, arrived to buy the Box of Secrets. One more fool who thought they would be the one to find the wisdom promised by the ancient legends.

And later, when the broken shell of a person brought it back, wanting only to stop seeing the images that filled their mind day and night, she would buy it back for a fraction of what they had paid for it.

They told her there was a mirror inside, a mirror that showed every evil thing man was capable of, all visible in the face of the person looking into it.

Funny, though. When she opened the box she saw no mirror. She saw nothing inside. Nothing but a name she was sometimes called.

Pandora.

THE END

CONCLUSIONS

"I have been thinking all day, and I've come to a conclusion," he said.

"Go on," she said.

"I'm in love with someone else."

"Really?"

"But the good news is that I'm still in love with you too!"

"Oh?"

"I love you deeply. It's just. . ."

"Yes?"

"It's just that I can't be limited to one person. I have a big heart, and I can love many people at the same time."

"I see."

"I can't limit myself. I'm a feeler. I empathize with women. It's natural for me."

"A feeler."

"And women love me. They hit on me all the time. I can't help it. You must have noticed, but you've been so good about not getting jealous."

"I suppose."

"So, I had this idea, and I'm sure you'll be okay with it."

"Yes?"

"I was thinking that my girlfriend, Sheila, the one that I'm in love with?"

"Go on."

"I thought she could just move in with us. She needs a place to stay, and we have room, so I thought, what's the big deal? I know it's hard to spring this on you so sudden. . . "

"Yes."

"It's okay, you can think about it. I know it's a lot to ask. It's just that I told her I'd call her with the news, and she's expecting me to. . . have you decided? You have that look on your face like you've decided something. Am I right?"

"Yes. I've come to a conclusion."

She pulled the revolver from her purse and fired. The bullet hit him square between the eyes and knocked him back on the sofa. His brains splattered on the wall behind, like a hunk of raw hamburger. His mouth was twisted in a grimace that could have been fear, or perhaps anger.

She stared at him for a moment, then went over and folded his arms across his chest.

"That's better."

Now he had the look of someone who had come to a conclusion.

THE END

THIS WON'T HURT A BIT

"Mr. Huxley, it looks like I have to fill one of those back teeth today," the dentist said, looking up from his chart.

Jerry Huxley squirmed in the dentist's chair. He had never liked visits to the dentist, not since he was a little child, and it hadn't gotten easier now that he was in his 40s.

"Sure, doc," he said. "Just make sure you numb me first, okay?"

"Of course, Mr. Huxley," the dentist said. He was a small man with a smooth professional manner and brilliant white teeth.

Jerry talked a lot when he was nervous, and he chattered on now as the dentist got the needle ready.

"You know, I had an uncle once who swore his dentist put radio receivers in his fillings, and that the government was trying to control his mind that way," he said. "He was crazy, of course. Imagine, thinking something like that."

The dentist chuckled. "I'm afraid our technology hasn't progressed to that point," he said. "Now, just relax. This won't hurt a bit."

Jerry flinched while the dentist inserted the needle, then slowly relaxed as he took it out.

"Yeah, Uncle Joe was crazy," he said. "Delusional. He had all sorts of theories about what they were trying to do to him. Poor guy ended up in a mental institution. He said he couldn't stop hearing voices in his head."

"Is that so?" the dentist asked. He stepped on a pedal and opened a stainless steel trashcan, then threw the empty cartridge from the hypodermic needle into it. "What type of work did he do?"

"Oh, he led a simple life. Never married. Worked nights as a security guard. He spent his days in the library, though, surfing the Internet or poring over old books. He had all sorts of theories about UFOs, government conspiracies, cover-ups, you name it. He was a conspiracy nut, I guess you'd say."

"I know the type," the dentist said. "The ones who think the government is behind everything bad that happens.

"Yeah, that's it."

"They come up with the craziest ideas."

"You can say that again. My uncle certainly had some nutty ideas. And he had boxes of papers in his apartment, file cabinets full of 'research' that he said proved he was right. Pictures, even."

"Really?" the dentist said. "What ever became of it?"

"Oh, it's all in my basement. I cleaned out his apartment when he had to go in the mental institution, and I just put it in the basement. He begged me not to throw any of it away, and I just couldn't bring myself to go against his wishes. Even though I knew he was crazy. He's been dead a few years now, though, and I made a resolution to clear it out. I'm sure I'll get a chuckle reading through that stuff."

"How is your mouth feeling? Is it numb yet?"

Jerry probed around with his tongue. "Yep. Can't feel a thing."

"Good. I'll get to work, then." The dentist moved efficiently about his work, humming a pleasant tune. He had an annoying habit of talking while Jerry's mouth was full, though, and Jerry couldn't answer.

"It certainly is a pity that people get these crazy ideas about the government," the dentist said. "Why, the government is just trying to protect us. It's an evil world out there. They're just trying to do the best for us." His voice was serene, although there was a vein in his neck that throbbed as he spoke.

Jerry wanted to make a joke about how that's exactly what Uncle Joe said we should watch out for -- the attitude that the government knows best. But of course he couldn't, because the dentist was probing around in the back of his mouth with his instruments.

In less time than Jerry expected, the dentist was finished. "All done," he said. "I'm very happy with the work I did. You can rinse, and then be on your way."

"That was fast, doc," Jerry said, rubbing his mouth. "And it doesn't hurt at all."

"I used a very powerful anesthetic," the dentist said. "You may feel a bit woozy for a few hours, but that's to be expected. Everything will be fine in the end."

Jerry shook the dentist's hand, happy that it was over. In minutes he was outside, whistling a happy tune as he looked for his car in the parking lot. It was, "Don't Worry, Be Happy". It occurred to him that he hadn't heard that song in awhile. Now I won't be able to get it out of my head for days, he thought. That's what always happens with catchy tunes like that.

Inside, the dentist stepped into a room at the back of the office suite and closed the door. He sat down at the desk, reached in his mouth and pulled his false teeth out, then put them on the desk. He reached in a drawer of the desk and took out a black, official-looking cell phone. He punched in a few numbers, then a few more numbers when he heard the automated voice prompts. Then a live voice came on the line.

"Yes?" the voice said.

The dentist leaned his head back, opened his mouth wide, and made gurgling noises from deep within his throat.

"Speak English, please," the voice said.

"Sorry, Eminence," the dentist said. His voice sounded liquid, like water sloshing. "I did an implant today."

"Oh?"

"On a 43 year old white male named Jerry Huxley. I did his uncle 20 years ago. His name was Joe. You have him on record."

"The name is familiar. I thought he was deleted."

"Yes. He left a paper trail, though. This nephew has all his records."

"I see. I'll notify Security. Good work."

"Thank you." The dentist grinned, his toothless maw opening wide. "I do my best to fight disease when I see it."

THE END

SIN OF THE FLESH

"Flesh? You mean to say people in the future expose their flesh?" Darcy said.

"They are nearly naked on the beach. I saw it with my own eyes." Professor Smythe pursed his lips disapprovingly.

"Such immorality! They must have no sense of decency."

"Quite. It made me long for the example of our dear Queen Victoria, who is the pillar of modesty. Which is why I have decided to hide my time machine. The future is an immoral time, not fit for anyone of our era to see."

"Yes, but in the interest of Science, perhaps a trip or two. . ."

"No! Those sights are not meant for men's eyes. I will lock up my invention and that is final."

"As you wish."

Later, though, Darcy snuck into the carriage house, took the tarpaulin off the machine, and started it. He told himself he was doing it for Science. He couldn't remember which year his friend had told him he visited. No matter, he simply set it for several hundred years in the future.

The machine whirred and clanked, it's wheels and rotors spinning into life. They spun faster and faster, and the air seemed to shimmer and blur. Then, everything stopped, and Darcy saw sand, and heard the nearby surf.

What luck! He was on a beach, and would be able to see--

Something bit into his shoulder, and he was jerked out of his seat and up in the air. He found himself dangling ten feet up, staring into the eyepiece of a shiny metallic thing that seemed to be studying him. There was a whirring sound coming from the region behind its eyes. Another sharp claw sliced through his clothing, and in seconds he was naked. The thing examined him more closely, touching his flesh with another appendage that had long, cold fingers.

"What is it?" a voice from below said. "What have you found, Rex?"

Darcy looked down and saw a squat, black thing looking up at him, from a group of other squat black things. They looked like enormous beetles. Somehow, they could talk, although he didn't know where their voices were coming from.

He was suddenly lowered almost to the ground, where the beetle things could see him with their large insect eyes. Their antennae swayed back and forth, and the sun reflected off their smooth black shells.

The first voice said: "Interesting case. Most of them don't try to camouflage themselves anymore. Their mating rituals require nakedness."

"Disgusting," the rest said, in chorus. "Get it away!"

Darcy wanted to cover himself, but he could not. Then he was raised high in the air and flung hard to the ground. He broke several bones, and was in an agony of pain.

The last thing he heard before being crushed to death by the droid's 10 ton foot, his insides splattered across the beach, was: "Sorry that you all had to see such an obscenity on our beach. We've eradicated most of them, but there are still a few stragglers."

THE END

DON'T YOU JUST LOVE WEDDINGS?

"Look at Sis's new husband," Lilith said. "He's smiling."

"He won't be later," said Ted.

"You survived our wedding night."

"Just barely." Ted stroked a scar on his cheek. "Any chance she's different?"

"We're sisters, silly. It's genetic."

"Right. Poor guy."

"Was it that bad, Pookie?" she purred.

"Bad? Finding out on your wedding night that sex turns your wife into a--"

"This conversation is getting me hot. Let's go upstairs." She pulled him up by his tie.

"Have a great night, you two," Lilith said, winking at the bride.

"Welcome to the family," Ted said to the groom.

THE END

HEART STOPPING BEAUTY

The sign in the window said, "Gone fishin'", and Christopher Van Meter felt a wave of fear rise in him. It was the only jewelry store in this godforsaken town, and he needed to get his watch fixed fast.

It had stopped, and he could feel the change happening already.

He had always been so careful about not getting stuck like this. And then he thought of Daria, who was back up the hill at the hotel. God, she was beautiful: jet black hair and green eyes, and that little ghost of a smile. It had promised so much, that smile. It had warmed him, made him forget the pain in his soul, enticed him to end his long bachelorhood. He had never gambled, not once, until her. "You only live once," she would say, and he'd thrill to her randy kisses in an elevator, or a park, or a busy street.

He heard the shout of a child, and he turned to see a boy riding his bike around the cobblestone circle at the center of town. Around and around he rode, shouting from the sheer joy of being alive. There's eternity for you, Van Meter thought. Ticking clocks don't exist for him. But he, Christopher Van Meter, was bound by space and time. He was stuck in a village in upstate New York, on his honeymoon, and the jewelry store was closed. His watch had started slowing down yesterday, but he couldn't think of it then -- Daria took up all his time. Early in the morning he had awoken to stiffness in his joints, and he knew before looking that the watch was stopped. He'd tiptoed out of the room and walked as fast as he could down here to the town square.

Now he realized he'd have to drive someplace else, find another town with a jeweler who was open. It was his only recourse. Daria wouldn't understand, so he'd just have to leave. He'd make up a story -- an appointment, an emergency, had come up -- if he ever saw her again. He looked back up the street, winding up to the hotel perched like an Alpine chalet on top of the mountain. The effort it would take to walk up there and get the car would fatigue him.

But that boy riding his bike around the square. Look at all the energy he had! Christopher lifted his arm and waved laboriously, and the boy pedaled over.

"Can you help me?" Christopher said, with a voice that sounded like a creaky hinge.

"What do you need?" the boy said.

"A taxi. Do you know where I can get a taxi?"

"Old man Jones runs a taxi service. Over on the other side of town."

Christopher's heart leaped. "Can you ride over and ask him to come here? I want to use his service. I'll give you a quarter."

"A quarter? That's not much money."

"What? Why, when I was a boy. . ."

"That was a long time ago, Mister."

And Christopher realized it was. "Okay. I'll give you a dollar." He reached in his pocket, and held out a dollar in his trembling hand. The boy's eyes lit up, and he snatched the bill. "That's more like it.

It'll only take me ten minutes." And he took off. Christopher sat down on a bench. The sun was rising in the sky, beating down on his head, but Christopher's bones felt chilled. How long was ten minutes? The boy couldn't possibly know. Once, he had been that way - the days were endless. Now he could count the seconds by the spots appearing on his hand.

It was weakness to let a woman turn his head. But oh, he had never felt so alive.

When the taxi drove up, the white haired old man behind the wheel got out and looked around. He couldn't see anything but an old-fashioned vest pocket watch on the bench. "That Pierce boy ought to get a whipping," he said out loud. "Taking me away from my crossword puzzle, just to play a joke." He picked up the watch and held it up to the light. The numbers were in some language he'd never seen before. "Well, it's not a total loss," he said. "Somebody'll pay a good price for this at the outdoor market next Saturday." He got back in the cab, slammed the door, and drove off. A handful of dust whirled in the breeze as he sped away.

THE END

PRIME CUT

"This is a wicked good steak," Joey said. "Where'd ya get this meat, Angie?"

"You like it?"

"I love it. I never tasted nothing like it."

"I got it from the supermarket. They have a new butcher in the meat department. He's such a cute guy, blonde wavy hair, ice blue eyes. And so helpful. The kind of guy who really listens to a girl, and tries to help her out. Anyway, he has the best meat."

"Yeah, well, that's good, Angie. I'm glad you found a new friend. Now, listen, I'm gonna tell you something, but I don't want you to cry. I hate it when you cry."

"What's that, Joey?

"I got a new girlfriend. Her name's Honey, and she has a body on her like a damn Mack truck. I mean, she has curves on top of her curves. She has skin like, you could bounce a quarter off it."

"You used to say that about me, Joey."

"I can't help it, Angie, I'm in love with her. You're not crying are you?"

"I'm not crying, Joey."

"That's a switch. You always cry when I tell you about a new girlfriend."

"I'm over that, Joey. I mean, after the 200th time, a girl gets used to it. Well, maybe not used to it, so much. You want another piece of steak?"

"Yeah, sure. This is the best meat I ever had. So what was it you were saying?"

"Nothing, just that I decided crying don't do no good. I mean, what good did it ever do me to cry about you cheating on me on our wedding night? Or the time when I was in the hospital after my car accident, and you couldn't come to see me right away because you had a date?"

"Angie, I told you, I promised that girl I'd take her out. I didn't want to break a promise."

"I know, I know. Here's your steak. Good, isn't it?"

"Better than the first one. I better finish this fast, though. I gotta date with Honey tonight. Funny thing, she hasn't answered her cell phone all day."

"I'm sure she'll turn up eventually, Joey."

"Yeah, I guess so."

"Now, here's a nice little salad I made you."

"Angie, you know I don't like salad."

"Joey, it's good for you. You don't eat enough salad. Besides, I fixed this one special."

"Yeah, looks like you put some crazy new vegetables in it. What are these things, anyway. They look like little pink carrots, except -- what the? Is this a finger? What is this, a joke? It's a joke, right? And wait, is this a ring? Oh my god, that's the ring I just gave Honey!"

"Remember that nice butcher I told you about? Well, it turns out he's a whiz with a knife. Oh, I'm sorry, Joey. Was there something wrong with the meat? You look like you have an upset stomach, sweetie. You're turning all green."

THE END

THE SMELL OF LOVE

Wallace was 35 and lived with his mother. He was an entomologist, and it was more than a day job to him. He came home from work and spent hours in his basement lab, studying the mating habits of wasps, the way worker bees communicate, the whole concept of pheromones, and how insects will act different ways based on the pheromones they sense in the air.

His mother Betty didn't understand it, but she liked that he was still living with her. She ran a perfume shop in town, and she told her customers, "He can't get married; he has to take care of me when I get old."

Plus, she didn't think any girl was good enough. Most girls, if you took away the makeup, the clothes, and the perfume, what were they? Not much, she thought.

When Wallace brought Apis around the first time, his mother hated her. Apis was a scientist too, who worked at Wallace's company. She had thick black glasses and mousy brown hair and big white horse teeth. She wore clunky shoes and no makeup and dresses that didn't fit her.

Wallace's mother was appalled. The girl didn't even try to fix herself up. Amazingly, though, Wallace was madly in love with her. Betty noticed the look in his eyes when he was around Apis. It was a look she hadn't seen before. He even started wearing a minty aftershave, and he got his messy hair cut.

Then, he started not coming home at night. He would call and say he was staying at Apis's.

That's when his mother started spending time in his basement lab, reading his books and studying his insects.

She learned all about pheromones.

One day, Wallace told her he was taking Apis on a picnic for her birthday. He wanted to give her a present.

"I have just the thing," Betty said. "A bottle of perfume. I have a lovely scent in the store that would be perfect for her."

Wallace wasn't sure if Apis wore perfume, but he finally agreed.

The next day Betty gave him a little red box with a gold bow on it. "Give it to her when you're at your picnic," she said. "She'll love it."

So a day later Wallace gave Apis the little bottle while they were sitting on a blanket having a picnic lunch. She blushed, and gave him a peck on the cheek, and then opened it and said it was perfect, so sexy. It smelled earthy, honeyed, even a bit peppery. She put a little dab behind each ear, and one down between her surprisingly perky breasts.

Wallace looked at her with adoration.

He was so entranced with her that he did not hear the noise behind him, which was like a hundred cars with engines that were making that noise when you can't get them to start. That gnashing, grinding noise.

That angry, buzzing noise.

It got louder, but Wallace still didn't seem to hear it. All he could do was look at Apis with love and lust in his eyes.

Apis was facing the forest behind Wallace, and she saw something like a black cloud coming out of it.

"What's that coming out of the woods?" she said, squinting through her thick glasses. "It sounds like a lot of very angry wasps, but why would they--"

Her fingers went to her ears, and to her chest. To the places where she'd put the perfume spiked with pheromones by Wallace's mother.

THE END

TICK TOCK

"**I** am 540 years old," the girl said. She had long blond hair, and empty blue eyes. She didn't look a day over 21.

"Oh?" Lillith said. "Have you learned anything in that time?"

"I'm bored," the girl said, pouting. "I can't feel anything anymore."

Those were the magic words. They meant that the prospect was willing to part with an obscene amount of money for the ultimate high.

"Sign here," Lillith said, handing over the contract. Funny how science had achieved so much, including immortality, but an old-fashioned pen and paper were needed to enforce a contract under the law.

The girl signed, expensive bracelets jangling as she did. "What now?" she asked, after signing her entire fortune over to Lillith.

"Come with me." Lillith led the way to the back of the shabby store, past a curtain and down a shadowy hallway. At the end of the hallway, she opened a door and ushered the girl into a room with an ancient hospital bed in it, and some medical equipment in a corner.

"Lie there," Lillith said, pointing to the bed.

"Will this hurt?" the girl said.

Lillith chuckled. "Of course it will hurt. You're perfection itself, honey. You've had the best of everything your whole long life. Money, drugs, education, beauty, fame, sex, knowledge -- you've had it all. It's not enough, though, is it? Everything gets boring after awhile. That's why you came to me. You heard I can make you feel again, right?"

"Yes. I haven't cared about anything for a century or more."

"You want to feel fear, right? Terror."

A light went on in the girl's eyes. "I heard it's the strongest emotion. A real rush."

"Yes it is," Lillith said. "But there's no turning back, sweetie."

"I understand."

Lillith inserted the needle deftly into the girl's arm, and emptied its contents into her vein.

"What is terror? Can you describe it?"

Lillith smiled. "Have you ever played the Slasher Game?"

"Yes, many times. Is it like that?"

Lillith smiled again. "Nothing like that. Because once the game was over, you came back to life, right? Your body repaired itself, so even if you had gotten your throat cut, it was just like taking a little nap, and then you woke up."

"Yes."

Lillith laughed. "Terror, real terror, is nothing like that. You will learn what it is now." She threw the needle in the trashcan, and went over to the sink to wash her hands.

"I feel different," the girl said. "Strange."

"That's normal," Lillith said, wiping her hands with a paper towel. "Your body is changing. That's part of the process."

The girl got off the bed, and went over to the mirror above the sink. She peered at her face. "Something is different."

"Yes. It's the beginning of terror. Your body is reacting to it."

The girl seemed to have a tremor in her voice. "I, I don't like it."

"Nobody said you would like it, honey."

The girl gripped the sink, hard, like she was trying to stop the shaking in her body. "What's happening?" she said.

"You'll get used to it. It's known as aging. It used to be a common thing, many centuries ago."

"I, I want my money back," the girl gasped. Her face was ashen, and she was shivering. "C-c-cancel the contract."

Lillith smiled. "Impossible. The contract is irrevocable."

"No!" the girl screamed. "No! Please! I didn't think it would feel this way. I can't handle this. Please, you must understand. My face looks different." She put her hands to her ears. "Oh my God. . . what's that noise? What is that horrible noise?"

Lillith smiled and pointed to a contraption on a table by the door. It was a historical object, stolen from a museum, and Lillith had paid a lot of money for it on the black market.

"That?" she said. "Why, that's the ticking of a clock."

THE END

THE RETURNING

June 6, 1789

Annabelle Lockard woke from a dream-filled sleep with a start. There had been a sound. What was it? Her mind cleared, and she remembered. It was a thump, downstairs in the maid's quarters. There was moonlight streaming in through the open window, and she could see the hands on the clock standing like a sentinel by the door - two o'clock.

A pain lanced her heart as she realized what the sound was. She choked off a sob, and her insides tightened as she pulled the sheets back and sat on the edge of the bed. The curtains fluttered in the cool breeze, and she shivered and reached for her robe from the chair next to the bed.

There were only a few dying embers in the fireplace, and she pulled the robe tightly around her and cinched it. She walked quietly to the door and opened it, then tiptoed down the hallway, careful to step over the creaky floorboards. The door of the bedroom at the end of the hall was open, and as she suspected, the big four-poster bed was empty. The sheets were pulled back, and when she put her hand on them they were still warm. There was a whiff of ginger in the air - Duncan's scent, and she remembered how that smell enveloped her when she put her head on his shoulder.

But he was not here. He had betrayed her again, and her insides went cold with rage. This time she would not brush it away - this time, she would embrace it. She walked back down the hallway to her room, and found her way in the dark to her dresser table, where her expensive French perfumes were. She opened the stopper on one, her favorite, the one that smelled of roses. She dabbed it around her neck, drinking in the smell.

She moved carefully down the stairs, one step at a time. There were muffled sounds coming from the back of the house. Each one drove a dagger through her heart. When she got to the bottom of the stairs, she turned and saw herself in the big mirror at the opposite end of the room, over the mantel. She was like a phantom, her hair standing out wildly from her head, her hands trembling, a mad glint in her eyes. On the mantel was a painting, a full-size portrait of Duncan, sitting astride his horse in his blue officer's uniform, gold braid on his shoulders, with the smile of a man who threw caution to the wind.

How many times had she seen that cocksure smile in the ensuing years? The smile that said, "I will betray you, darling, and do it before your very eyes."

And he had betrayed her, countless times, in broad daylight, in front of their friends, her parents, strangers - it made no difference. The man was without shame. It was a good thing they'd had no children.

She heard another sound, this time louder. She'd heard it often from him in the early years of their marriage - a low growl, building to a tone of urgency, a tone of imploring, a tone of wild abandon. To hear that tone now, coming from that trollop Katie Flynn's quarters, was one more insult added to all the others.

Under the painting was the sword he'd been awarded for his service for America, after he'd left the British army and switched sides at the battle of Yorktown. She went over and took it off the hooks, and thrilled to its heft in her hand. She tightened her fingers around the hilt, and strode through the room, then past the kitchen, and down the long narrow passageway to the maid's quarters, her heart pounding as the sound, that wild moaning sound, got louder and louder.

At the door, there was the scent of ginger. She burst in, saw them in the bed, their bodies writhing like dogs, faces covered with sweat and lust, and she was on them in an instant, the sword slashing into flesh and bone, the first blows disabling them, and the many blows that came after only serving to turn them into bloody, featureless masses on the bed.

She did not know how long it went on, only that she was soaked with sweat and panting hard when she heard a scream behind her, and she turned and saw the cook, in her nightgown, her hands covering her mouth in horror at the bloody scene. Reason, sense, came back to her, and she realized the cook would run and tell the neighbor down the road, Squire Edwards and his family, and that she would surely be hung for this crime. Better to save them the trouble. She went back to the great room, took the sword to Duncan's picture, slashing it to ribbons in an instant, then, staring at her bloody image in the mirror, she swung the blade hard into her neck, slicing it to the bone, and fell to the floor. As she died, she saw a light coming toward her.

***

June 6, 2010

They skulk into the room cautiously, like burglars. The boy's flashlight scans the room, revealing nothing but dust and cobwebs. There is no furniture, just a broken down fireplace and a mantel.

This is creepy," the girl says. She has a tight grip on the boy's hand.

"There's nothing here," he says. "It's just an old house. My family has owned this land for a long time. The original owner was somebody way back in my family. A soldier during the Revolutionary War. They say he was murdered here."

"Stop, Bobby," the girl says, hitting him on the arm. "You're scaring me."

The boy shines the flashlight under his chin, giving him a ghastly look. "Whoo," he says, in a high-pitched voice, "the ghost is coming to get you."

"I told you to stop," the girl says, pouting.

"All right," the boy says. "Let's forget about ghosts." He drops the flashlight to the floor and kisses her. Her body is pliant, and she responds to his roving hands with a soft moan.

They are locked in an embrace when Annabelle comes down the stairs. but she hardly notices them. They are nothing to her. Her passion is in the back room; her mind is there. There have been others like these two over the years, and she has brushed them aside like fleas from the sleeve of a dress.

"What's that funny smell?" the girl says, breaking free. "Like something rotten. Like, rotten flowers."

They turn and see her now, and they both gasp. She is coming toward them, her white gown covered in blood, her hair like Medusa's, her eyes rolling in her head.

"Bobby," the girl says. "What. . ."

But she has passed directly through Bobby, and he is lying on the floor twitching, his heart spasming from the shock, the evil current that has passed through it.

She has no concern for them; she must go and find Duncan, repeat the ritual. She walks to the back room, the sword still in her hand, deaf to the girl's screaming, her calls for mercy, her boyfriend's twitching face.

THE END

John McDonnell believes in the power of imagination and language to transform life. He has done many types of writing, but fiction is closest to his heart. He writes in the horror, sci-fi, romance, humor and fantasy genres. He lives near Philadelphia, Pennsylvania with his wife and four children.

Discover other titles by John McDonnell at Amazon.com and Smashwords.com.

Visit John McDonnell's Website at www.johnfmcdonnell.com

Did you like this book? Connect with John by email: mcdonnellwrite@gmail.com.

Printed in Great Britain
by Amazon

55192057R00026

13 HORROR STORIES

John McDonnell

ii